Rudolph
the
Red-Nosed Reindeer

and

Rudolph Shines Again

Robert L. May

Illustrated by Marion Guild

Follett Publishing Company
Chicago

Library of Congress Catalog Card Number: 64-21581

Rudolph the Red-Nosed Reindeer

'Twas the day before Christmas, and all through the hills
The reindeer were playing, enjoying their spills.

While every so often they'd stop to call names
At one little deer not allowed in their games.

"Ha ha! Look at Rudolph! His nose is a sight!
It's red as a beet! Twice as big! Twice as bright!"

While Rudolph just cried. What else could he do?
He knew that the things they were saying were true!

Where most reindeer's noses are brownish and tiny,

Poor Rudolph's was red, very large, and quite shiny.

In daylight it sparkled (The picture shows that!)

At nighttime it glowed, like the eyes of a cat.

Although he was lonesome, he always was good—
Obeying his parents, as good reindeer should!

That's why, on this day, Rudolph almost felt playful.
He hoped that from Santa, soon driving his sleighful

Of presents and candy and dollies and toys
For good little animals, good girls and boys,

He'd get just as much (and this is what pleased him)
As the happier, handsomer reindeer who teased him.

So as night, and a fog,
hid the world like a hood,

He went to bed hopeful;
he knew he'd been good!

While way, way up North, on this same foggy night,

Old Santa was packing his sleigh for its flight.

"This fog," he called out, "will be hard to get through!"

He shook his round head. And his tummy shook, too!

"Without any stars or a moon as our compass,

This extra-dark night is quite likely to swamp us.

To keep from a smash-up, we'll have to fly slow.

To see where we're going, we'll have to fly low.

We'll steer by the street lamps and houses tonight,

In order to finish before it gets light.

Just think how the boys' and girls'
hopes would be shaken

If we didn't reach 'em
before they awaken!

Come, Dasher! Come, Dancer! Come, Prancer and Vixen!

Come, Comet! Come, Cupid! Come, Donder and Blitzen!

Be quick with your suppers!
Get hitched in a hurry!

You, too, will find fog
a delay and a worry!"

And Santa was right, as he usually is.
The fog was as thick as a soda's white fizz.

He tangled in treetops again and again,

And barely missed hitting a huge, speeding plane.

Just not-getting-lost needed all Santa's skill—

With street signs and numbers more difficult still.

He still made good speed, with much twisting and turning,

As long as the street lamps and house lights were burning.

At each house, first checking what people might live there,

He'd quickly pick out the right presents to give there.

"But lights will be out after midnight," he said.

"For even most *parents* have then gone to bed."

Because it might wake them, a match was denied him.

Oh my, how he wished for just *one* star to guide him!

Through dark streets and houses old Santa did poorly.

He now picked the presents more slowly, less surely.

He really was worried! For what would he do,

If folks started waking before he was through?

The night was still foggy,

and not at all clear,

When Santa arrived

at the home of the deer.

Onto the roof,

with the clouds all around it,

He searched for the chimney,

and finally found it.

The room he came down in

was blacker than ink,

He went for a chair,

but it turned out ... a sink!

The first reindeer bedroom
was so very black,

He tripped on the rug,
and burst open his pack.

So dark that he had
to move close to the bed,

And peek very hard
at the sleeping deer's head,

Before he could choose
the right kind of toy—

A doll for a girl,
or a train for a boy.

But all this took time, and filled Santa with gloom,

While feeling his way toward the next reindeer's room.

The door he'd just opened—when, to his surprise,

A soft-glowing red-colored light met his eyes.

The *lamp* wasn't burning; the light came, instead,

From something that lay at the head of the bed.

And there lay—but wait now— what *would* you suppose?

The glowing, you've guessed it, was *Rudolph's red nose!*

So *this* room was easy!

This one little light,

Let Santa pick quickly

the gifts that were right.

How happy he was, till he went out the door . . .

The *rest* of the house was as black as before!

So black that it made

every step a dark mystery.

And *then,* came the greatest

idea in all history!

He went back to Rudolph and started to shake him,

Of course very gently, in order to wake him.

And Rudolph could hardly

believe his own eyes!

You just can imagine

his joy and surprise

At seeing who stood there,

a paw's length away,

And told of the darkness

and fog and delay,

And Santa's great worry that children might waken

Before his complete Christmas trip had been taken.

"And you," he told Rudolph,

"may yet save the day!

Your bright shining nose, son,

can show us the way.

I need you, young fellow,

to help me tonight,

To lead all my deer

on the rest of our flight."

And Rudolph broke out into such a big grin,

It almost connected his ears and his chin!

He scribbled a note

to his folks in a hurry.

"I've gone to help Santa," he wrote.

"Do not worry."

Said Santa, "Meet me and my sleigh on the lawn.

You'd stick in the chimney." And flash, he was gone.

So Rudolph pranced out through the door, very gay,

And took his proud place at the head of the sleigh.

The rest of the night . . . well, what would you guess?

Old Santa's idea was a brilliant success.

And "brilliant" was almost no word for the way

That Rudolph directed the deer and the sleigh.

In spite of the fog, they flew quickly, and low,

And made such good use of the wonderful glow

That shone out from Rudolph at each intersection

That not even once did they lose their direction!

At all of the houses and streets with a sign on 'em,

The sleigh flew real low, so Rudolph could shine on 'em.

To tell who lived where, and just what to give whom,

They'd stop by each window and peek in the room.

Old Santa knew always which children were good,

And minded their parents, and ate as they should.

So Santa would pick out the gift that was right,

With Rudolph close by, making just enough light.

It all went so fast, that before it was day,

The very last present was given away.

The very last stocking was filled to the top,

Just as the sun was preparing to pop!

The sun woke the reindeer
in Rudolph's home town.

They found the short message
that he'd written down.

Then gathered outside
to await his return.

And were they surprised
and excited to learn

That Rudolph,
the ugliest deer of them all,

Rudolph the Red-Nosed,
bashful and small,

The funny-faced fellow they always called names,

And practically never allowed in their games,

Was now to be envied by all,
far and near.

For no greater honor

can come to a deer

Than riding with Santa and guiding his sleigh.

The Number-one job, on the Number-one day!

The sleigh, and its reindeer, soon came into view.

And Rudolph still led them, as downward they flew.

Oh my, was he proud as they came to a landing

Right where his handsomer playmates were standing.

The same deer who used to do nothing but tease him
Would now have done *anything,* only to please him.

They felt even sorrier they had been bad
When Santa said, "Rudolph, I never have had

A deer quite so brave or so brilliant as you
At fighting black fog, and at steering me through.

By YOU last night's journey was actually bossed.
Without you, I'm certain, we'd all have been lost!

I hope you'll continue to keep us from grief,
On future dark trips, as COMMANDER-IN-CHIEF!"

While Rudolph just blushed, from his head to his toes,

Till all of his fur was as red as his nose!

The crowd clapped their paws and then started to screech,

"Hurray for our Rudolph!" and "We want a speech!"

But Rudolph, still bashful,

despite being a hero,

Was tired.

His sleep on the trip totaled zero.

So that's why his speech was quite short, and not bright,

"Merry Christmas to all, and to all a good night!"

AND that's why— whenever it's foggy and gray,

It's Rudolph the Red-Nosed who guides Santa's sleigh.

Be listening, this Christmas, but don't make a peep,

'Cause that late at night children *should* be asleep!

The very first sound that you'll hear on the roof

That is, if there's fog, will be Rudolph's small hoof.

And soon after that, if you're still as a mouse,

You may hear a "swish" as he flies 'round the house,

And shines enough light to give Santa a view

Of you and your room. And when they're all through,

You may hear them call, as they drive out of sight,

"Merry Christmas to all, and to all a good night!"

Rudolph Shines Again

'Twas a month before Christmas, when Rudolph, at play,

Saw Santa drive up, to call from his sleigh:

"The weatherman says there'll be snow Christmas Eve.

So please tell your parents I'd like you to leave,

To lead all my deer through that dark, snowy night,

With your shining red nose and its wonderful light.

Meanwhile, of course,

you can work on the toys

We'll be taking, this Christmas,

to good girls and boys."

As Rudolph was hitched up in front of the rest,

He heard the deer whisper, "What makes him the best?"

"We're bigger and stronger!" "And older!" "You said it!"

"But we get the backaches, while he gets the credit!"

The deer in the workshop were mean to him, too.

They gave him the messiest glueing to do.

He carried the heaviest loads of them all.

And when football was played, they made Rudolph the ball!

Poor Rudolph! He worried, he wept, and he whined.

And the more he shed tears, the less his nose shined!

"Oh, poor little me," he would pity and pout . . .

Till one day, the light in his nose just went out!

"With this nose, I never could lead Santa's sleigh!

I'm useless here now . . . so why should I stay?

I'll leave here tonight while the rest are in bed,

And go to some faraway country instead,

Where none of the new folks who'll be introduced-to-me

Know how much brighter my nose really used-to-be!"

He left, and he traveled, for mile after mile . . .

Till one day, when ready to rest for a while,

In a field with a very thick forest behind it,

He heard a strange noise! But he just couldn't find it

Until he came closer, for darkness was falling.

Hundreds of rabbits were crying and calling:

"Two of our children, Donnie and Doris,

Taking a walk, got lost in the forest!"

"It's much, much too dark now to search or to follow them!"

"By morning, a fox or a wolf will have swallowed them!"

"If only we rabbits had eyes like a cat!"

"Or a bright shining flashlight; we sure could use that!"

Thought Rudolph, "These rabbits have reason to worry!
I'd better stop pitying me in a hurry!"

And right then and there, Rudolph ended his habits
Of pouting and tears, and thought just of the rabbits.

"I'll find them," he shouted. "I'll find Don and Doris
With my bright shining nose!" And he dashed for the forest!

Completely forgetting
himself and his woes,

He'd even forgotten
the change in his nose!

Because he was running
as fast as he could,

When he learned his mistake,
he was deep in the wood!

He now faced the risks
of that dangerous place

With a nose no more bright
than the one on your face!

"I promised the rabbits
their babies I'd save.

I may have been stupid;
I've got to be brave!

My nose doesn't shine,
but like all other deer's,

It's still a good sniffer;
I still have sharp ears."

Quickly and quietly, he ran through the forest . . .

Sniffing and listening for Donnie and Doris.

(And sniffing and listening, too, for the sly

Foxes and wolves that he knew were close by.)

With all that huge forest

to search, and no light,

Do you think that Rudolph

will find them that night?

Perhaps it was smartness;

perhaps it was luck.

Or perhaps a reward

for his bravery and pluck

Was sent by an angel,

from 'way 'way up high,

Who steered Rudolph's feet

toward a very small cry

From a thick patch of bushes.

And that's where he found them,

Frightened, but safe . . .

with leaves piled around them

To keep out the cold,

and wild animals, too.

"I'm your friend,"

Rudolph whispered.

"I've come here for you,

To help you get home.

So please have no fears!

Just jump on my back, and hold tight to my ears.

The foxes and wolves here would all like to meet us,

In order to cook us, and carve us, and eat us!"

So Rudolph bent down, and the bunnies obeyed.

He then ran so fast that no animal laid

A claw or a tooth on the bunnies or deer.

(Though two panting wolves came just terribly near!)

Then out of the woods . . . for a grand, happy landing

In the field where the crowd of sad rabbits were standing.

Just picture the Mother-and-Dad-Rabbits' joy,

When Rudolph brought back both their girl and their boy!

They thanked him and thanked him,

and begged him to stay.

Said Rudolph:

"I'll come for a visit some day.

But my job is with Santa, to help as I can.

I was wrong to go 'way from that wonderful man.

Perhaps it was 'cause of my weeping and whining

That all of a sudden my nose stopped its shining!

With a dull nose, last night in the woods, I helped you.

In that case, I surely could help Santa, too!

As Santa's front reindeer,

I guess I'm all through.

But I still could load boxes,

or work with the glue."

As tears from the rabbits' eyes started to roll,

He started his trip for the far-off North Pole.

Before this remarkable journey was through,

'Twas the day before Christmas! And darker it grew.

The gray northern sky and the fog and the snow

Would make almost anyone travel real slow,

Or even get lost! But Rudolph just flew . . .

Straight as an arrow, and speedily, too,

Through the heaviest snowstorm and fog of the season!

How did he do it? Can you guess the reason?

Ever since Rudolph had saved the young rabbits,

Forgetting himself, and ended his habits

Of thinking of Rudolph, and weeping and whining,

The light in his nose had again started shining!

At first very little . . . too dimly to view with it.

(Do you think that the angel had something to do with it?)

Then slowly more bright,

like a red glowing coal,

Until, when at last

he could see the North Pole

And Santa's big sleigh by the workshop front door,

It shone just as brightly as ever before!

The deer were all hitched; the sleigh almost loaded . . .
And Santa so worried, he nearly exploded:

"Without Rudolph's red nose and its wonderful glow,
How will I steer through the fog and the snow?"

But when he saw Rudolph,
he shouted, "Hurray!

Quick, take your place
at the head of the sleigh!"

The deer crowd called, "Rudolph, we deer are glad, too!"
"We hope you'll forgive the big loads." "And the glue!"

"For next year your job in the shop is a dandy!
Next year, your job will be tasting the candy!"

So happy young Rudolph led Santa's great sleigh,

With Rudolph's red nose again lighting the way

Through darkness and fog, to deliver the toys

That were given that Christmas to good girls and boys.

Swiftly they traveled . . . as Rudolph's nose shone

On each waiting chimney . . . including your own!

The very first sound you could hear on the roof,

As Santa's sleigh landed, was Rudolph's small hoof.

Then his nose made the light that gave Santa a view

Of you and your room. And when they were through,

You might, too, have heard, as they drove out of sight:

"Merry Christmas to all, and to all a good night!"

How Rudolph Came to Be

Robert L. May was born in 1905 in New Rochelle, New York. Like those of his famous red-nosed friend, Mr. May's early years were rather unhappy. Contemporaries found him too small to "belong", and even at college, he was too young and small to excel at anything other than scholastic achievement.

But Robert May's story has a happy ending even so, for, in 1939, he was asked to write "an animal story in verse" for his company. He created the Christmas classic RUDOLPH THE RED-NOSED REINDEER, which has come to be loved as one of the most popular Christmas stories ever written.

The creation of Rudolph, like most creations, was a step-by-step process of suggestion and elimination. Mr. May first had to decide on an animal for the story. He considered several, but finally chose a reindeer believing that it best symbolized the Christmas season. The plot? An "Ugly Duckling" who rises above his handicap to save the day. How does he accomplish it? Mr. May thought it *should* be because of the same differentia that made him the "Ugly Duckling" in the first place.

In Mr. May's words: "Separate analyses of Santa's needs and a reindeer's anatomy eventually pin-pointed the idea of the shining red nose that would be a foggy-night asset to Santa, but something *less* than a social asset to the youthful deer."

The rest is history. Rudolph has continued to grow in popularity until today he is as well-known and loved as Santa himself.